Chinese Americans

Our Cultural Heritage

SPIRIT
of America®

Chinese AMERICANS

By Lucia Raatma

The Child's World®
Chanhassen, Minnesota

Chinese AMERICANS

Published in the United States of America by The Child's World®
PO Box 326 • Chanhassen, MN 55317-0326 • 800-599-READ • www.childsworld.com

Acknowledgments
   The Child's World®: Mary Berendes, Publishing Director
   Editorial Directions, Inc.: E. Russell Primm, Emily Dolbear, Sarah E. De Capua, and Lucia Raatma, Editors; Linda S. Koutris, Photo Selector; Image Select International, Photo Research; Red Line Editorial and Pam Rosenberg, Fact Research; Tim Griffin/IndexServ, Indexer; Chad Rubel, Proofreader

Photos
   Cover/Frontispiece: A group of Chinese-American children dressed for Chinese New Year in New York City, 1911
   Cover photographs ©: Bain News Services/Corbis; Roger Ressmeyer/Corbis
   Interior photographs ©: Ann Ronan Picture Library, 6, 7 top; AKG-Images, Berlin, 7 bottom; Getty Images, 8; Corbis, 9 top, 9 bottom; Getty Images, 10; Culver Pictures, 11 top, 11 bottom; Corbis, 12, 13 top, 13 bottom; AKG-Images, Berlin, 14; Corbis, 15; TRIP/H. Rogers, 16; AKG-Images, Berlin, 17; TRIP/S.Grant, 18; Corbis, 19, 21, 22; TRIP/H. Rogers, 23 top; Corbis, 23 bottom, 24; AKG-Images, Berlin, 25 top; Corbis, 25 bottom; Getty Images, 26, 27 top; Reuters/Popperfoto, 27 bottom; Corbis, 28.

Registration
   The Child's World®, Spirit of America®, and their associated logos are the sole property and registered trademarks of The Child's World®.
   Copyright ©2003 by The Child's World®. All rights reserved. No part of this book may be reproduced or utilized in any form or by any means without written permission from the publisher.

Library of Congress Cataloging-in-Publication Data
   Raatma, Lucia.
   Chinese Americans / by Lucia Raatma.
         p. cm.
   Includes index.
   Summary: Introduces the customs, heritage, and traditions of Chinese Americans.
   ISBN 1-56766-149-1 (library bound : alk. paper)
   1. Chinese Americans—Juvenile literature. [1. Chinese Americans.] I. Title.
   E184.C5 R23 2002
   973'.04951—dc21
                              2001007805

Contents

Chapter One	The Ways of China	6
Chapter Two	Life in a New Land	10
Chapter Three	At Home in America	16
Chapter Four	The Chinese-American Culture	22
	Time Line	29
	Glossary Terms	30
	For Further Information	31
	Index	32

Chapter ONE

The Ways of China

THE CHINESE WERE AMONG THE FIRST GROUPS of **immigrants** who came to the United States during the 19th century. Before the late 1840s, few Chinese people lived in the United States. But all that changed in 1848 when gold was discovered in California. People in China, as well as in other countries, saw America as a place to become rich.

China is one of the world's oldest **civilizations**. It is believed that people lived in China as early as 5000 B.C. For thousands of years, **tradition** and family structure were very important in China.

Many Chinese citizens came to California in search of gold.

Women were expected to serve men and give birth to sons. Chinese society was disciplined and strict. Chinese men and women worked hard in rice fields and at raising families.

With the arrival of Europeans in the 1500s, China changed. The Europeans bought such goods as silk, spices, and tea from the Chinese. In the early 1800s, to pay for goods from China, some British traders smuggled a drug called **opium** into the country and sold it illegally. This drug can be used as medicine in some circumstances, but it is addictive. Many people in China took opium as a drug and often committed crimes to get it. The effects of the drug on China's health and economy were terrible, so China tried to stop the Europeans from bringing it into their country. This led to the Opium War of 1839 to 1842. The British

In China, working long days in rice fields was the way many made their livings.

Opium being smuggled over a town wall during the Opium War between Great Britain and China

Interesting Fact

▸ Between 1840 and 1900, approximately 2.4 million Chinese people left their homeland for America and other countries.

Conditions of extreme poverty led many Chinese to make a new life in America.

won easily, and China lost control over its own land. The Chinese had their independence taken away from them, and European influence over China increased greatly.

When the people of China got to know the Europeans, they learned about different customs and other ways of life. They began to listen to Western ideas about religion and culture. To some, China suddenly seemed like a harsh place to live. When the peasants waged war on government officials, China became dangerous for everyone. Also, floods caused large numbers of farms to fail. Many Chinese lived in dreadful poverty and didn't know how to make a better living. Some people began to think about moving to other lands, but few expected to leave China forever. Instead they hoped to make some money and then return to China to enjoy a more comfortable life. But many of those who left China during the 1800s never went back.

Paper Sons

THE SAN FRANCISCO EARTHQUAKE OF 1906 was a disaster for many people, but it opened doors for some Chinese newcomers to America. The earthquake and its fires destroyed many immigration records (left). As a result, some Chinese men got false documents stating they were born in the United States. Because children of American citizens were allowed to enter the United States, these false documents allowed the newcomers to return to China and bring back young men who claimed to be their sons. In most cases, of course, these men were not sons at all. Some were friends and some were distant relatives. In Chinatown, these young men were called "paper sons."

As they tried to enter the United States, the paper sons were held at Angel Island (below) for questioning. Officials asked them questions about their home and neighborhood in America. The young men had memorized information about these places, which they had never even visited before, of course. Usually they convinced the officials that they belonged in America, and they were allowed to enter.

Chapter Two

Life in a New Land

LEAVING CHINA WAS NOT AN EASY DECISION for most people. But once they set their sights on America, the Chinese worked hard to get there. They saved money to buy transportation across the Pacific Ocean, and often they had to leave their homes in secret. For many years, the Chinese government threatened to kill people who tried to leave the country. The trip across the ocean was extremely long and hard, but these

Panning for gold in California seldom brought riches to the Chinese, but many stayed and found work in other industries.

10

immigrants believed they were going to a better, richer place.

Sadly, many of the ideas that immigrants had about America were unrealistic. They hoped to find the streets paved with gold and to gather great wealth. Instead, when they arrived in California, they found that not everyone was getting rich during the gold rush. As miners, they often earned only $2 a day, but even that was a higher wage than they got in China. Few people found gold, and as the mines closed, the Chinese found other ways to make a living.

Many Chinese Americans opened laundries and restaurants, and they worked long hours. Unfortunately, many of the European immigrants who had come to America began to resent the Chinese. They thought the Chinese were taking jobs away from other newcomers. Soon, life in America became hard for the Chinese.

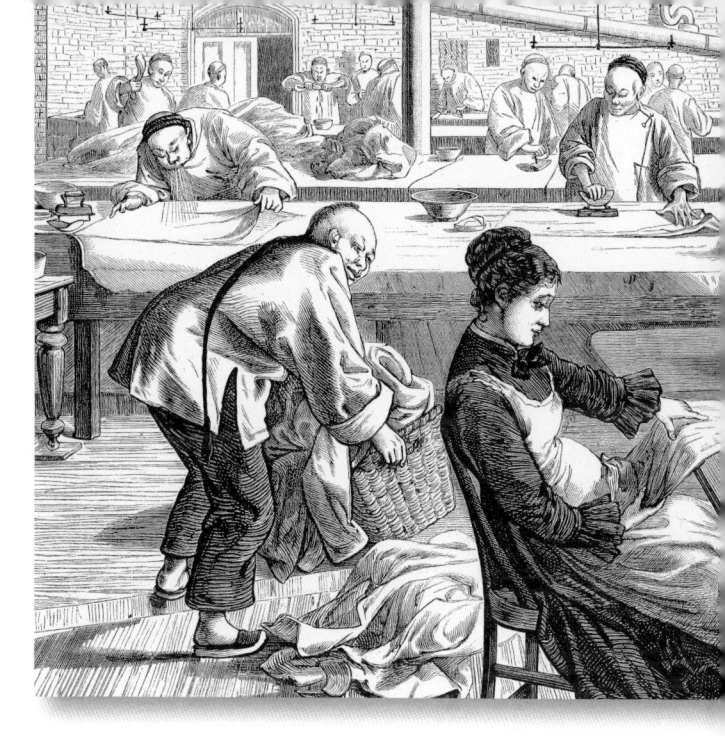

Some Chinese Americans began their own laundry businesses.

Chinese Americans played an important part in the building of railroads in the United States.

The former detention center on Angel Island is now the Asian Immigration Museum that teaches visitors about the history of Asian Americans in the United States.

Interesting Fact

▸ Most of the Chinese who came to America during the 1800s came from the Guangdong and Fujian Provinces.

In spite of these attitudes, the Chinese stayed. They played a key role in the building of the **transcontinental railroad** in the United States and they worked 14-hour shifts, often earning only $1 a day. Many Chinese laborers died while building the railroad, and their bodies were buried alongside the tracks. The railroad companies were not concerned about the health and safety of these workers. They simply wanted the railroad to be finished. When the railroad was finally completed in 1869, no Chinese workers were thanked or honored. Their backbreaking work went unnoticed by the United States.

As the years passed, conditions for Chinese Americans worsened. The Chinese Exclusion Act, passed in 1882, banned Chinese laborers from entering America. When new immigrants docked in San Francisco, California, they were often met by angry, fearful Americans. They were held at a small building called "the shack" for questioning and inspection.

From 1910 until 1940, Chinese newcomers to America were taken to Angel Island in San Francisco Bay, where they were held for days—and sometimes for months. Housing on the island was cramped and dirty, and many Chinese died there, never getting the chance to succeed in America.

These new Chinese immigrants were held at "the shack" before being allowed in the country.

The Chinese who were allowed to enter the United States faced other problems. Because they looked different from European immigrants, they were often called names and mistreated. Some people said that the Chinese were uncivilized, that they acted like animals. These attitudes were unfair and untrue.

Once in America, many Chinese settled into fishing villages.

Despite the **prejudice** they faced, Chinese Americans proved to be determined and strong. They found jobs

13

Interesting Fact

▶ Hiram Fong was the first Chinese American to serve as a U.S. senator. He represented the state of Hawaii from 1959 to 1977.

At work in the markets of San Francisco's Chinese community

in California's vineyards, in the fishing industry, and in garment factories. They showed the United States just how smart and **innovative** they could be. They even helped build more railroads throughout the Northwest.

Over the years, the Chinese formed their own communities. They continued to practice their own religious customs and to eat their traditional foods, including rice, soy, fish, and bamboo shoots. A neighborhood in San Francisco became known as Little China. Before long, sections called Chinatown sprang up in cities all over America.

In 1943, the Chinese Exclusion Act was **repealed** and, in 1965, all restrictions on Chinese immigration were removed. People from China were finally welcomed to America. In recent years, many Chinese have decided to leave the **communist** government of China, and their migration to the United States continues today.

Chinese Religions and Philosophies

THE TRADITIONAL religions and **philosophies** of China include Buddhism, Confucianism, and Taoism. Buddhism began in India thousands of years ago, and later spread to China and other parts of Asia. Buddhists believe in living simple lives, free from attachment to material things. They believe in respecting other people, and they believe in **reincarnation**.

Confucianism is a system of ideas based on the teaching of Confucius. This wise Chinese **philosopher** believed in respecting the older generation, keeping the family together, and obeying people in authority.

Taoism is based on ideas taught by Chinese philosopher Lao-tzu. Taoist philosophy stresses the importance of harmony between people and nature.

15

Chapter THREE

At Home in America

Chinese Americans made their homes in New York's Chinatown and in neighborhoods all over the country.

IN THE 1950S, MORE CHINESE WOMEN BEGAN arriving in the United States. Some brought their children. Many were finally reunited with their husbands. At last, Chinese-American families began to thrive in their new nation.

Chinese Americans moved to cities and communities throughout the United States. Today, many live in Los Angeles and San Francisco, California; New York City; Seattle, Washington; and Chicago, Illinois. They also settled in smaller towns throughout the nation. In these communities, they have become strong forces in education, encouraging excellence in their children.

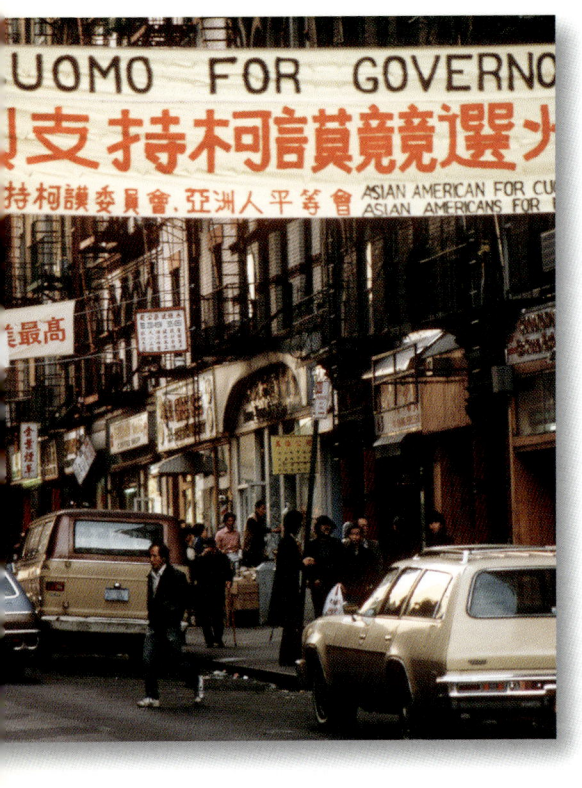

Chinese art accompanied by writings in the Chinese alphabet

As soon as Chinese immigrants arrived in the United States, they struggled to learn English. This was a real challenge, because the Chinese and English languages do not use the same alphabet. The Chinese were often teased for their way of pronouncing certain words, but they worked hard to learn the language of America.

Some Americans of Chinese background continue to practice Buddhism and other Eastern religions. Many others, however, have adopted Christianity. Some Christian

Interesting Fact

▶ An Wang, founder of Wang Laboratories, was a leader in the computer industry for many years.

Colorful parades mark the celebration of the Chinese New Year.

Interesting Fact

▶ During the 19th century, 90 percent of the Chinese who came to America were men.

churches and temples hold services in Chinese today.

Family members are still an important part of Chinese-American life. Children are taught to respect their parents and grandparents, just as they are in China. Holidays such as the Chinese New Year are celebrated with joy—as well as with dragons and colorful parades.

Today, many Chinese Americans still face unfair treatment in the United States. Many are paid less than their white coworkers, and sometimes companies are slow to promote

Chinese Americans to management positions. Groups such as the Organization of Chinese Americans and Asian Americans for Equal Employment work to ensure equal rights for America's Chinese citizens.

In spite of the unfair treatment they have experienced, however, Chinese Americans have overcome the prejudice and hatred they first experienced. They have studied hard and gone to college, married, and raised families. They have become scholars and scientists, physicians and firefighters, attorneys and authors. No matter what reactions they received from a society that didn't always welcome them, many Chinese have embraced the United States as their home.

Interesting Fact

▸ For hundreds of years, Chinese men wore their hair in long, thin braids called queues (kyooz).

Today Chinese Americans work in all kinds of businesses.

Tiananmen Square

IN JULY 1989, MORE THAN ONE MILLION CHINESE COLLEGE STUDENTS did something very brave—and very dangerous. They staged a demonstration in Tiananmen Square in Beijing, China. Many of the students had visited the United States and studied there. They called for a democratic government and demanded an end to communism in China.

The Chinese government was angered by the demonstration. Officials sent the Chinese military to end it. Several hundred students were killed. Many more were taken to prison.

People around the world were shocked and saddened by the events that took place that day in Tiananmen Square. Many Chinese students who were attending colleges in the United States were afraid to go home. They worried that they too would be imprisoned or killed. A large number of these Chinese students chose to stay in America and help make their new country a better place.

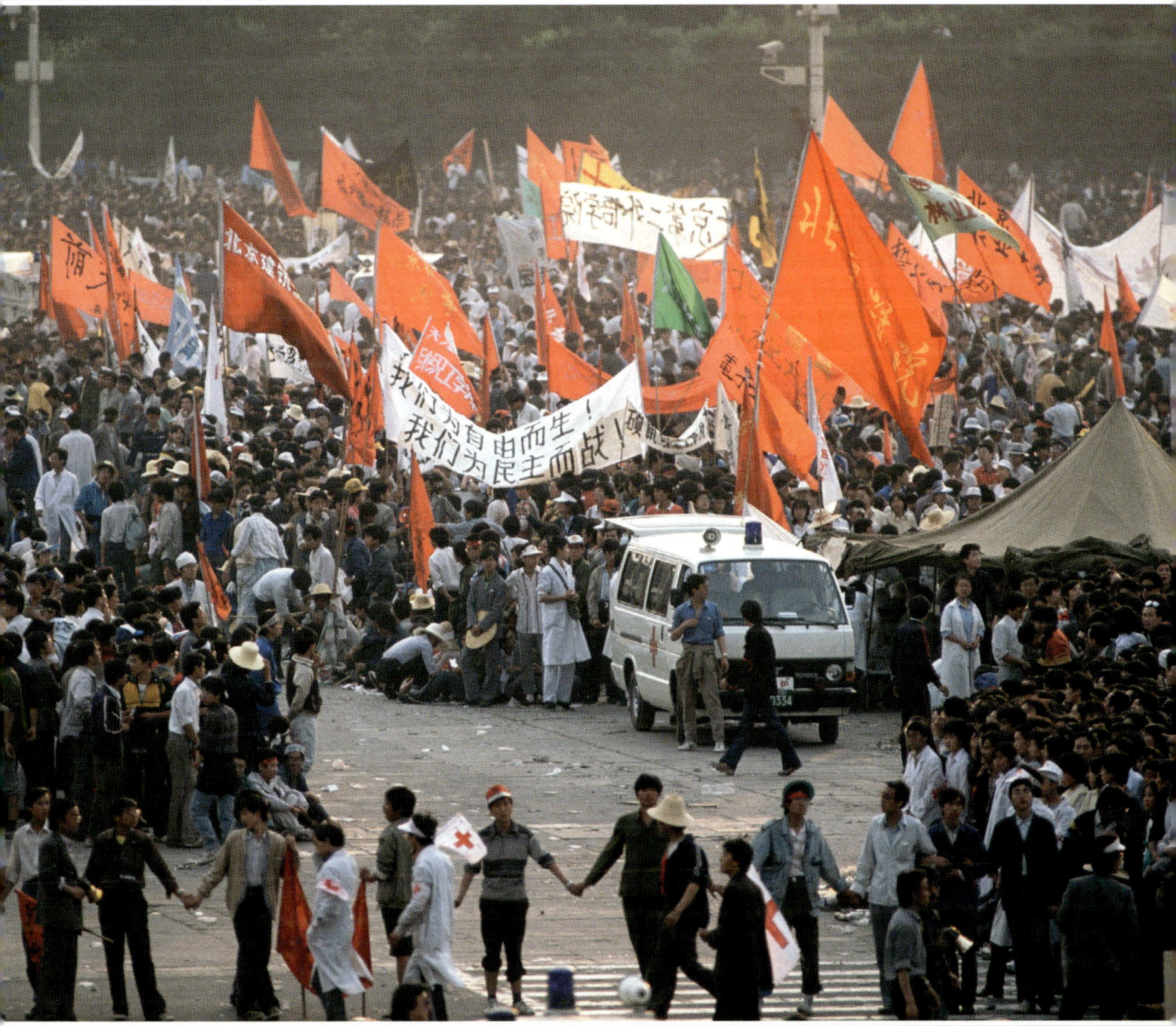
我们为自由而生！
我们为民主而战！

Chapter Four

The Chinese-American Culture

THANKS TO THE CHINESE, AMERICANS FROM all backgrounds have been introduced to unique ideas, customs, and food. Oriental rugs, porcelain items, and china dinnerware are found in homes across the United States.

Chinese porcelain is quite beautiful and graces homes throughout the world.

Many people follow the ideas of feng shui, which is the ancient Chinese art of placing objects. When items such as furniture and decorations are positioned in certain ways, they are said to bring harmony and good luck.

Americans of all ages enjoy the paper-folding

art of origami. Many historians believe origami began in China shortly after paper was invented there in A.D. 105. Meanwhile, in kitchens and restaurants from coast to coast, Americans enjoy Chinese specialties such as chow mein, fried rice, egg rolls, wontons, and fortune cookies.

Americans of all backgrounds enjoy dining in Chinese restaurants (above) and often end their meals with fortune cookies (below).

23

Architect I. M. Pei has designed famous structures throughout the world.

Interesting Fact

▸ When a communist government took power in China in the 1950s, about 5,000 Chinese students and professionals were stranded in the United States. Afraid to return home, most of them remained in America.

Chinese Americans have added to the U.S. culture in other ways, too. Actress Ming-Na was born in China but moved to the United States with her family when she was four years old. She was the voice of the title character in the animated film *Mulan*, and she stars on the television drama *ER*. Actor Bruce Lee brought martial arts to mainstream America in such films as *Enter the Dragon*. On television, Connie Chung gained fame as a broadcast journalist.

Architect I. M. Pei is known for designing buildings and cities throughout America and the world. Some of his projects include the National Center for Atmospheric Research in Boulder, Colorado; the John Hancock Building in Boston, Massachusetts; the East Building of the National Gallery of

Art in Washington, D.C.; the John F. Kennedy Library in Boston; and the Rock and Roll Hall of Fame and Museum in Cleveland, Ohio.

Another important architect is Maya Lin. While still a student at Yale University, she designed the striking Vietnam Veterans Memorial at the National Mall in

The Vietnam Veterans Memorial in Washington, D.C. (above), was designed by Chinese American Maya Lin (below).

25

Washington, D.C. Several years later, she was chosen to design the Civil Rights Memorial in Montgomery, Alabama.

Amy Tan is the author of *The Joy Luck Club* and *The Kitchen God's Wife*, as well as books for children. She grew up in California and is the daughter of Chinese immigrants. She continues to tell wonderful stories about China. Other notable Chinese-American writers include Maxine Hong Kingston, Wing Yung, and J. S. Tow.

In sports and recreation, Chinese Americans have contributed as well. Tennis player Michael Chang won the French Open in 1989 and has continued to achieve success in the sport. Americans of all ages have taken

Author Amy Tan tells stories about China and about Chinese Americans.

up **tai chi chuan**, a disciplined yet relaxing form of exercise.

In the field of health, Chinese medicine has made great contributions. Many ideas about using herbs to cure and treat sickness originated in China. Now these practices are being adopted all over the world. And the ancient art of **acupuncture** has helped many Americans deal with pain and illness.

Music lovers throughout the world enjoy the work of cellist Yo-Yo Ma. This talented musician began playing the cello as a child. As a young man, he studied at the Julliard School in New York City.

The United States boasts a wonderful mixture of people. Its population is

Michael Chang won the French Open tennis tournament when he was just 17 years old.

Cellist Yo-Yo Ma has gained an audience throughout the United States and the world.

Interesting Fact

▶ American attitudes toward Chinese people changed during World War II (1939–1945) when China became an **ally** of the United States.

Tai chi chuan is a disciplined and relaxing form of exercise.

made up of Europeans and Asians, Native Americans and African-Americans. All these people have brought customs and ideas to the United States. All have contributed to make our nation what it is today. Chinese Americans have contributed new ideas about health and exercise. They have also brought delicious food and joyous celebrations. And, above all, they have shown themselves to be a smart and courageous group of men and women—people who have made America a better place to live.

Time Line

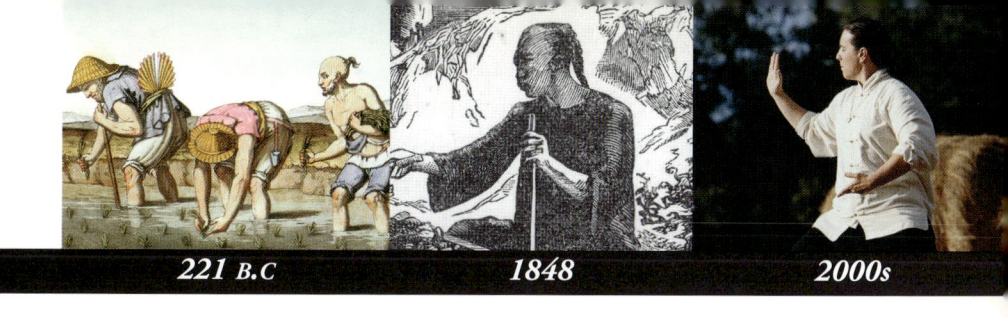

221 B.C   **1848**   **2000s**

221 B.C The ruler of the Ch'in dynasty establishes himself as the First Emperor. The name of this dynasty serves as the basis for the word China.

1500s European traders arrive in China.

1800s British traders smuggle opium into China.

1839–1842 China fights the British in the Opium War but is defeated.

1848 Gold is discovered in California; the first wave of Chinese immigration begins.

1860 The state of California creates segregated schools because government leaders feel white children should not be in the same classroom with other races, including Chinese.

1869 The transcontinental railroad is finished.

1882 The Chinese Exclusion Act is passed.

1900 The census taken this year shows that there is only one Chinese woman for every 26 Chinese men in the Unites States.

1906 The San Francisco Earthquake destroys immigration records, allowing more Chinese immigrants to claim citizenship and bring friends and relatives over from their homeland.

1910–1940 Chinese immigrants are held and questioned at Angel Island.

1930 Japan begins to take steps to conquer China.

1939–1945 World War II occurs. China is an ally of the United States, and 16,000 Chinese Americans serve in the U.S. military

1943 The Chinese Exclusion Act is repealed.

1950 Chinese Americans start creating anti-communist organizations after communist leaders take over their homeland.

1959 Hiram Fong becomes the first Chinese American to win a seat in the United States Senate. He represents Hawaii until 1977.

1965 All restrictions on Chinese immigration to America are lifted.

1979 The Chinese are the third largest group of people who immigrate to the United States each year.

1989 Hundreds of Chinese students are killed by the government during a pro-democracy demonstration in Beijing's Tiananmen Square.

Glossary Terms

acupuncture (AK-yoo-pungk-chur)
Acupuncture is a Chinese system of inserting small needles at certain points in the body to relieve pain and certain illnesses.

ally (AL-eye)
An ally is a person or a country that helps another, usually in war. China was an ally of the United States during World War II.

civilizations (civ-ih-lih-ZAY-shunz)
Civilizations are groups of people who live and work together in a community. China is one of the world's oldest civilizations.

communist (KOM-yuh-nist)
A communist is a person who believes in the system of government called communism. In this system, the government owns all industries and property. China's government is communist.

immigrants (IM-ih-grents)
Immigrants are people who leave their own country to make a home in another country. The Chinese were some of the first immigrants to the United States.

innovative (IN-nuh-vay-tiv)
Innovative means to be modern and to come up with new ideas. The Chinese have always been innovative.

opium (OH-pee-uhm)
Opium is a drug that is used in several medicines; it is also addictive. In the 1800s, British smuggled opium into China.

philosopher (fih-LOSS-uh-fer)
A philosopher is someone who studies truth and wisdom. Confucius is a famous Chinese philosopher.

philosophies (fih-LOSS-uh-feez)
Philosophies are beliefs. Some of the philosophies of China are Buddhism, Confucianism, and Taoism.

prejudice (PREJ-uh-diss)
Prejudice is an unfair attitude toward a certain group of people. Chinese immigrants often faced prejudice.

reincarnation (ree-in-kar-NAY-shun)
Reincarnation is being reborn after death with a new body and earthly life. Buddhists believe in reincarnation.

repealed (rih-PEELD)
Repealed means overturned or abolished. In 1943, the Chinese Exclusion Act was repealed.

tai chi chuan (TIE-CHEE-CHWAN)
Tai chi chuan is a slow exercise that blends breathing with movement. Many Americans practice tai chi chuan.

tradition (tra-DISH-unz)
Traditions are customs that are followed for generations. Traditions are very important in Chinese culture.

transcontinental railroad (trans-kon-tih-NEN-tul RAYL-rohd)
A transcontinental railroad is a railroad that connects the east and west coasts of a continent. Chinese Americans played a key role in the building of America's railroads.

For Further Information

Web Sites

Visit our homepage for lots of links about Chinese Americans:
http://www.childsworld.com/links.html

Note to Parents, Teachers, and Librarians:
We routinely verify our Web links to make sure they're safe, active sites—so encourage your readers to check them out!

Books

Daley, William, and Sandra Stotsky. *The Chinese Americans.* New York: Chelsea House Publishing, 1995.

Hoobler, Dorothy and Thomas. *The Chinese American Family Album.* New York: Oxford University Press Children's Books, 1998.

Kite, Lorien. *The Chinese.* New York: Crabtree Publishing, 2000.

Olson, Kay Melchisedeck. *Chinese Immigrants, 1850–1900.* Mankato, Minn.: Blue Earth Books, 2001.

Wu, Dana Ying-Hui, and Jeffrey Dao-Sheng Tung. *The Chinese-American Experience.* Brookfield, Conn.: Millbrook Press, 1993.

Places to Visit or Contact

Chinese Culture Center of San Francisco
750 Kearny Street
San Francisco, CA 94108
415-986-1822

New York Chinatown History Museum
70 Mulberry Street, Second Floor
New York, NY 10013
212-619-4785

The Organization of Chinese Americans
1001 Connecticut Avenue, N.W.
Suite 601
Washington, DC 20036
202-223-5500

Index

acupuncture, 27
Angel Island, 9, 13
architecture, 24–25
Asian Americans for Equal Employment, 19

Beijing, China, 20
Britain, 7–8
Buddhism, 15, 17

Chang, Michael, 26
Chicago, Illinois, 16
children, 16
China, 6–8, 14, 15, 20, 23, 27, 28
Chinatown, 9, 14
Chinese Exclusion Act, 12, 14
Chinese New Year, 18
Christianity, 17–18
Chung, Connie, 24
communism, 14, 20, 24
Confucianism, 15
Confucius (philosopher), 15
customs, 8, 14, 22

education, 16, 19
employment, 11, 12, 13–14, 18–19, 24
Enter the Dragon (film), 24

families, 6–7, 16, 18, 19
farming, 7, 8
feng shui, 22
foods, 14, 22, 23
Fujian Province, 12

gold, 6, 11
Guangdong Province, 12

holidays, 18

The Joy Luck Club (Amy Tan), 26

Kingston, Maxine Hong, 26
The Kitchen God's Wife (Amy Tan), 26

language, 17
Lao-tzu (philosopher), 15
Lee, Bruce, 24
Lin, Maya, 25–26

literature, 26
Little China, 14
Los Angeles, California, 16

Ma, Yo-Yo, 27
martial arts, 24
medicine, 27
men, 7, 16, 18
Ming-Na, 24
mining, 11
music, 27

New York City, 16

opium, 7
Opium War, 7–8
Organization of Chinese Americans, 19
origami, 23

paper, 23
"paper sons," 9
Pei, I. M., 24–25
prejudice, 11, 12–13, 18–19

queues (braids), 19

railroads, 12, 14
religion, 15, 17–18

San Francisco, California, 14, 16
San Francisco earthquake, 9
Seattle, Washington, 16
sports, 26

tai chi chuan, 26–27
Tan, Amy, 26
Taoism, 15
Tiananmen Square, 20
Tow, J. S., 26
transcontinental railroad, 12

Wang, An, 17
Wang Laboratories, 17
women, 7, 16
World War II, 28

Yung, Wing, 26